Creatureville
The Broom Quest

Written by Terri Green
Illustrated by Terri Green

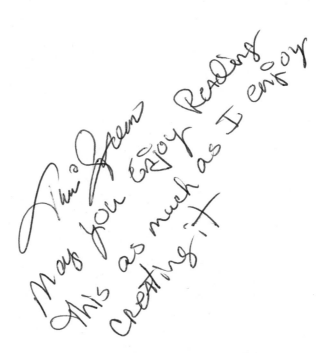

Contents

Creatureville
The Broom Quest

Written by Terri Green

Chapter 1
In the Beginning

Once upon a time, long, long ago. Well...... at least before there was cable television. There were three main TV channels, public access and maybe a local channel. Late at night on Friday or Saturday evenings about 10 PM, a show would come on called "Creature Feature". It would show old black and white monster movies, they were fun to watch. The old movies included, Frankenstein, and his Bride, The Mummy, Werewolves, and of course Dracula. The monsters were created or lived in small villages and towns. They would be chased out of them by the local villagers with pitch forks and torches blazing with fire. Some people would be armed with guns loaded with silver bullets. While others carried wooden steaks and large hammers. The wooden steaks would be driven into the hearts of the vampires, while they slept in their coffins. I always wondered what had happened to these wonderful monsters.

So I decided to set out to find them. After traveling over half of the earth on my quest. Look at those mountains, how tall they are. They are bigger than any mountains that I have come across so far. The sooner I get to them the sooner I can climb them. As I walk towards the large mountain range, I can see a small village up ahead at the base of them.

It's a good thing because it's almost nightfall. Maybe they will have a place for me to stay. The people here are very friendly and accommodating. The villagers all greet me with hand shakes and thank me for coming. They set up a large feast in the middle of the street, just for me and ask me to spend the night. It seems they rarely get visitors and want to show how thankful they are when they get one. I explain to all of them my story and what I am doing here. Everyone said they knew of no such creatures but want to help me any way they can. They gave me the best room in the tiny village. It's still pretty primitive, but it's better than sleeping on the ground outside.

As I'm getting ready to leave the next morning, an old man approaches me. He is very old and sort of stooped over with a long white beard and tattered clothes. He told me to stay away from the old castle and pointed into the distance. The old man warned me not to go anywhere near it because it was an evil place. It would be the end of me, for strange and wicked things happen there. All who attempts to go there never return. With a warning like that I have to go and see for myself. With the castle in my sights, I follow an old overgrown brick road until I come upon the old burned out castle. So they do know something of monsters but were afraid to tell anyone.

The large stone castle is overgrown with weeds and large

massive vines growing all over the walls. Parts of it has fallen down and the old stone seems to be crumbling away. Some of the damage is a result of a fire and other parts of it is from years of neglect. Pulling out my long sharp machete, I hack and chop my way through the vines, until the door way into the dark deserted building can be seen. The massive solid wood doors, that once stood proudly in the large opening, now hang crooked against the old dirty walls. The spider webs hang thick blocking the doorway and covering anything they can, like a blanket. I have to use my machete to cut through all of the webs in order to make my way through.

Entering the building, there is a large room, with a large stone staircase winding its way up to another floor. On each side of the stairs going behind the steps appears to be hallways. Also at each end of the room are two large arched doorways. Most of the stone walls in the room are blacken from the fire that happened so long ago. The floor is made of black and white marble in a checker-board pattern, it's littered with leaves, dirt and remnants of the old building. Pieces of a chandelier lay in the middle of the floor. Walking into the room, I decide to go to my left to the large archway at that end of the room. As I make my way across, the sound of dried leaves crunch under my feet. Looking up you can see that most of roof is missing. There is not much of it on the floor so it must of burned away.

Standing in the archway it's easy to see that half of the large room has fallen into a large hole underneath the castle. The front wall and part of the far wall has crumbled away. There seems to be part of a large fireplace and a couple pieces of broken furniture covered in white dust and webs in the back of the room. The walls and what is left of the floor are also blackened from a fire. This must have been the living room or drawing room.

 So I turn around and walk toward the first hallway closest to me. About halfway over to the hall, I stumble over some debris and fall flat on my face. While picking myself up off the floor I see a large hole in the floor that I almost step in. Must be more careful from now on. This hallway is very dark, luckily I have a flashlight in my backpack. The light shines on the walls and ceiling, but it's hard to see the floor. Better go around and try the other hallway first.

Walking past the stairs I look up and wonder if it would be safe to go up. Deciding to finish exploring this floor first, I must continue on to the next hallway. Shining the light in the dark narrow hall, I can make out the floor and what looks like a torch on the wall. Great, that will light up the hall much better than my flashlight. My lighter is in my pocket and easy to reach. The torch lights up quickly with the help of the cobs covering it. Great, there's a torch a little farther down the hall. I'll use that one and leave the first one lit to help find my way back. There are two doors on the left, one at the end of the hall and one on the right. The first door on the left is a closet. Door number two seems to be some kind of a storage room. There doesn't seem to be a lot of rooms on this floor but they are all oversized rooms.

At the end of the hall is a set of double wooden doors. I have to use all my body weight to push open the large heavy doors. They squeak and moan as I push them open. Once inside the room I can see that it's a library. Most of the walls are covered with shelves and books. A lot of the books are scattered on the floor and burned. There is a large oversize desk that is broken and sitting on its side in the middle of the room. The oversized fire place still has wood in it. Most of the windows in this room have no glass in them. The couple that do, are broken. There is broken glass laying all over the floor. As I turn around to go back out, there is an oversized painting of a man. It hangs crooked and has some rips and tears in the canvas. Stopping, I wonder who that could be a painting of.

 Continuing on down the hall to the last door. Carefully opening the door, it leads into what must have been a kitchen. There are cupboards, a table and an old wood-burning stove. There is another door at the head of the room. This must lead into the dining room. Walking through the kitchen I kick some old bowls and a pan out of the way. They make a loud clanging noise as I kick them, the sound echos though the empty building. Walking through this doorway, there are some broken chairs and part of a table. Looking over to my right is a large archway. That must be the archway I saw when I first entered the castle. As I walk over to the large doorway, I can see that it is and stroll back into the large foyer.

With the two lit torches maybe I can see down that other
hall. Retrieving the second lit torch I walk over to the
other dark doorway. Placing one of the torches in the
holder next to the door, now I can see the stairway going
downward. Carefully stepping on each crumbling stone,
holding onto the torch with one hand, and my other hand
on the wall. Slowly I make my way to the bottom step. In
the depths of the old castle, or what was left of an old
dungeon. To the left of me I can see some daylight and a
pile of fallen stones. That must be under the front room
that caved in, no need to go that way. Walking toward the
back of the dungeon I hear glass breaking under my feet.
There is a long table turned over on its side. Shelves and
cabinets pulled over, with all kinds of broken debris
laying on the floor everywhere. There is another heavier
table standing on one end, up against a wall. Why are
there straps on here? Look at all of the wires running into
those conductors that are attached to the table. This looks
like some kind of steel helmet, with wires running into
the top of it. I stop to study the debris on the floor, it
looks like test tubes and broken beakers laying
everywhere. This must be some kind of laboratory.
Walking yet further back into the dark creepy dungeon
there's a wall that just...doesn't look right. It's at the back
of the castle, up against the mountain itself. There's a
crack in it, that runs straight up and down. I decide to
push my hand against it...it moves. So I press harder, it's
looks like a secret passageway. Lets see where this goes.
Walking along in the tunnel for about one mile, I finally

find a cave at the end of the underground passageway. The cave is dark and gloomy. While hiking through the cave I find it necessary to hide from strange creatures and avoid horrible pitfalls. They are too scary and numerous to talk about. Finally reaching the other end of the cave, there is an opening. It's so dark, the only way that I could tell I was out of the cave was by the smell of fresh air. It's pitch black in this forest that the cave opens into. The density of this black forest is like none I have ever seen before. The earth is more water than solid ground. The sounds around me are creepy and scary. Sounds that no known creature could have made. Pushing my fears aside I continue on my quest.

Making my way through this horrible swamp is challenging as well as frightening. The mosquitoes are as large as small birds, I have to keep my machete in my hand to swat at them. Luckily my torch is still burning brightly, if it goes out I could be in real trouble. With the need to start walking a little faster, I must keep in mind there could be quick sand or drop offs that might put me in more danger. Since I can't tell if it's day or night I'll have to walk as long as I can. Finally, becoming so tired that there is no choice but to stop and sleep. Even though I found some hard ground, sleeping in the trees will be safer. Finally I find a good tree to climb with a branch large enough that I can lay on it. Sleeping with one eye open all night I was able to get some rest. Of course, I arose extra early in the morning, ate some jerky that I always carry and continue on my walk. Trudging through the dense forest as best I can for the next two days and nights, marking my trail as I go. Finally, on the third day, the forest seems to be getting a little lighter. The sun is starting to shine through the foliage overhead a little. Then all of a sudden, as if turning a light switch, the forest walls ended and a large open green field lay before my eyes. The sun shines brightly as far as the eye can see. All around the base of the large mountains that encircle this beautiful valley you can see the black forest, as if protecting the lush valley.

In the distance I could see what seems to be a small town. As I walk across the vast field there are pumpkins growing wild everywhere. There are all kinds shapes and sizes. They become thicker until there are so many of them I have to start walking over them and on them. What a beautiful sight, a sea of orange. At last there is a bit of a road that slowly starts to widen, as I get closer to a handmade stone bridge. The bridge looks just wide enough for a cart to cross it. There is a babbling brook running underneath the stone structure. The banks are braced with rocks along both sides of the small river and a wrought iron sign arched over the top of the bridge that says Creatureville.

It looks as though there is a house built into one side of the river bank under the bridge. A door and a window with a metal crooked smoke stack coming out of the side of the rocks. Exactly the same as all of the story books describe a Troll would live in. The closer I get to the small town, I start to see all types of houses, not much different than what you would see anywhere. They are all old, some are two story houses with big wrap around porches and ginger bread decorating them, as well as small crooked shacks. It's as if I've stepped back in time. A few horse drawn buggies and carts are traveling along the road. Some old jalopies and a couple of old pick up trucks are parked in front of some old houses, that look like they are from another place and time.

It seems to be a small town like any other you have ever heard of. With one traffic light in the center of it. A building on one corner with a fire station, a library in the back and the town hall upstairs. A corner drug store with a soda fountain sits on another corner. The local bank and post office share a building on one of the corners. On the fourth corner is a small diner, with a chalkboard in front announcing the day's specials. There is a dime store, a fixit shop and a small grocery store. These are just some of the shops in the quaint little town. Of course no town would be complete without a barber shop. Where old men of the town sit out front, gossip and tell old stories. Most of the buildings in town are made of dark red bricks with huge display windows in the front of them to show off their wares.

No one seems to pay any attention to me as I continue to walk through the small town. Even though I appear to be different from everyone here. The people here all look like the monsters from every monster movie I have ever seen. Over there, is that Count Dracula talking to the Mummy? Swamp Thing tips his hat at me as he passes by, I return the gesture with a nod. Continuing on, I turn right at the traffic light. Just past the firehouse on the other side of the old brick road, there is a large old gray stone building. Monster-looking children are walking to the building or are outside on the front lawn playing.

Wait, I can hear music playing. It seems to be coming from that stone tower, over on the right of me, there is a garage made of stone next to it.
With four teenage monsters playing a rock song with a sign on the base drums saying "The Beast". What, what is that noise, it sounds like a small engine backfiring and cutting out. Turning around to see where the noise is coming from, I jump out of the way into some bushes just as something whizzes by me. The noise continues to spit and sputter, suddenly, CRASH! BANG! CLANG!

"MOM!" yells Frankster, a teenage monster that looks like Frankenstein's monster. "Warren is flying in town again". Frankster checks out his guitar as he gets up off the floor. The microphone that Frankster was using lay on the ground, with his cool sunglasses laying next to it. Manly Werewolf, and his drums are knocked over, one of the cymbals is still spinning, making a ringing noise. His long golden hair that runs the length of his tall body is all tangled. "It's going to take me an hour to comb out my hair again. Thanks a lot Warren," Manly says sarcastically. Manly picks himself up and starts gathering up his drums and tries to set them upright again. Zack Dracula and his keyboard are knocked up against the wall. Roland, the second child of the Frankenstein's and the bass player, did manage to jump out of the way.

13

A funny looking truck pulls up in front of the stone tower. On the side of the truck it says "We Deliver, Milk, Eggs and Blood".

A very large and tall creature gets out of the van. Oh my he looks just like Frankenstein's monster himself. Could it be, no, but he is a descendant of the original Frankenstein. The top of his head is flat with bolt looking things coming out each side of his neck. He must be eight feet tall and his skin has a tint of green to it. "What's going on boys?" Pop Frankenstein asks the group. "Warren is flying in town again, and he crashed into us as we were practicing for the talent show," cries Roland as he gives his little brother an annoyed look. Roland is the biggest of all three Frankenstein boys. He is taller and built stockier or more muscular than even his older brother.

Pop looks down at his youngest boy and says, "Warren now you know that you are supposed to fly out of town in Pumpkin meadows. Son practice makes perfect, but you need to realize what your talents are. You may want to stop trying to become a warlock. You are not of magic decent, you are of human decent. But do remember quitters never quit, but never be afraid to quit." Warren looks up at his father and whines, "But Pop, I could fly better if I could get these training brooms off. Most witches and warlocks have theirs off before they start Kindergarten. Here I am well past that and I'm stuck trying to learn on this small broom. It's just to hard." Pop kneels down to his youngest son and says, "Son we've been through all of this before, you need to get better before I will get you a new broom. If you cannot control this smaller broom, how in the world will you ever handle a new bigger, faster broom."

A tall extremely thin woman with long black straight hair down to her ankles, walks out of the tall stone tower. She's carrying an armload of brown paper bags. Maw Frankenstein walks down the steps and tells everyone, "It's time to go to school, we will all be late. How would it look if the kindergarten teacher is late and I live right across the street. Here are your lunches, now let's go." "Honey," Pop says to his bride, "I'll be late for supper tonight, we have another meeting about the Founders Day Festival. This time of year makes it tough to be both the local milkman and the mayor at the same time."
"I know it gets really busy for you with everything that you need to do. I'll keep a plate warm for you in the oven." replies Maw. As she gets up on her tiptoes to kiss her husband.

The Frankenstcin boys all yell at the same time, "Maw, Pop, not in front of everyone." They all cover their eyes, turn and walk toward the school. Ernie Igor rides on a magic carpet up to Warren, they greet each other by slapping each other on the back. Ernie and Warren are the best of friends. They have always done everything together, they were even born together. Doctor Mummy and his nurse Mrs. Annie Bell Igor, were at the

15

Frankenstein's to deliver Warren. Annie Bell who was also expecting a child, suddenly went into labor. Poor Doctor Mummy had a busy night trying to deliver both children at the same time. Usually, if you see one child, you see the other. They celebrate their birthdays together as well as spend every waking moment together, or as much as their parents will let them.

Chapter 2
School Days

Everyone gets to school and settles into their seats. The morning announcements come over the intercom. "Testing, testing...may I have your attention please. Just a reminder, this Saturday will be opening day for the carnival. On Monday the school will be closed for the founder's day festival." You can hear everyone yell, and clap their hands, throughout the school, as it echos down the halls. "Quiet down, quiet down," the announcer continues. If you intend to be in the talent show, you must sign up no later than noon tomorrow. The auditions will be in the gym right after classes tomorrow. Good luck to you all."

Warren's second period class is Science. He's in the fifth grade. All of the elementary classes are on the first floor. But the science class is upstairs on the second floor, because that is where the laboratory is located. Professor Madly is an excellent mad scientist. He is a tall thin man with thick dark rim eyeglasses. His gray hair tends to stand straight up on its ends. When he gets angry he will grit his teeth, while talking through them and runs his fingers through his hair. Ernie Igor is Professor Madly's assistant. Ernie wants to be a lab assistant like his fore-fathers. "Now I want everyone to listen very carefully as I give you your instructions. Ernie will be handing out the ingredients," says Professor Madly as he walks around the room looking over the children's shoulders. "Be careful when adding your ingredients together. Do it exactly as I say. If it's done properly you should get a small explosion with a puff of smoke. The directions are on the board also, if you have any questions, ask."

The Professor continues his instructions. "Start with the swamp water, bring it to a rolling boil in your cauldron. As soon as its ready, drop in two bats eyelashes, crush the dried milkweed leaves, slowly add them, stir, then count to ten. Add the six bittersweet berries. Stir again, now very carefully, add one drop of crow's sweat and ".... Poof, poof, poof. "It sounds like everyone has it." PLOP! (There is music that sounds like a merry go round) bubbles flow up from Warren's cauldron, then suddenly, POP, POP, POP, POP.... and several butterflies fly around Warren's head and then out the open window.

The entire class room roars with laughter. Professor is visibly mad. He runs his hands through his hair, grits his teeth, and in a controlled voice, trying not to yell, "Warren, how many bats eyelashes did you use. I would say way to many. Warren stay after class." Ring.... the bell sounds the end of class. Professor Madly yells over the noise of chairs scratching the floor, "Everyone read pages 238 through 251, for a quiz tomorrow."

The old teacher turns to Warren, "if you want to be a warlock, you must learn how to follow directions to the letter. Being a Warlock is a very detailed oriented skill. Mixing potions and experiments is not just throwing stuff together. It's knowing what each ingredient does and what you can mix it with, most of all how much. Can you

tell me what happened to your experiment, Warren?"
"Uh...uh...I don't know. I did everything just like you said," Warren stammered. "Warren you will never be a Warlock at this rate. This is a prep class for becoming a witch or a warlock. Besides needing it to pass into the next grade. The only way you are going to be able to pass is do to extra credit. You have failed all of your experiment projects. Do the extra study problems at the end of this chapter and turn them in on Tuesday after the festival. If you don't you may be repeating this class again next year. Make sure you study for the quiz, you will need high scores on all of your tests in order to compensate for your lab grade. Here's a pass so you can get into your next class. Don't forget to study!" Professor Madly tells Warren angrily as he's runs his fingers through his hair again.

Warren walks into history class, late as usually. Professor Madly always seems to keep him late. Everyone is starring at him and giggling. Warren hands the pass to Mrs. Wolfgang, the historian for the town of Creatureville. Her coal black hair looks so dark it shines a tint of blue as the light hits it. She likes to wear it really big and kind of puffed out all over. She is an extremely small woman about four foot tall and very slender. Because of her tiny size some of the kids try to push her around when they first start in her class. They find out quickly that big explosions come in very small packages. "Late again from Madly's science class? Hurry and sit down you are holding us all up. "All the children laugh. "Quiet down, quiet down. Everyone turn to chapter 13 in your history books. Can anyone explain what Founders Day is?"

Little miss know it all Tilly Troll jumps up and down waving her hand saying, "I know, I know!" Tilly Troll has bright orange hair, she always wears it in pigtails that tend to stand straight out each side of her head. Her skin is a bright lime green color, with big round pink cheeks and bright yellow eyes. Mrs. Wolfgang nods her head at Tilly allowing the young girl to speak. "It's the day that we celebrate the finding of our town."

"Yes, that is correct Tilly." says Mrs. Wolfgang, "How long ago was our town founded?" Again Tilly jumps up and down waving her hand in the air wanting to answer the question. Mrs. Wolfgang ignores her and looks around the room and asks, "Does anyone else know the answer? Who else would like to try. How about you, Warren?"

Warren stands up slowly and says, "It was founded by The monster Frankenstein over 100 years ago."
"Come now Warren surely you know the year closer than that,"says Mrs. Wolfgang. "Can anyone else tell me exactly how long ago it was?" (Tilly jumping up and down now saying, "Please let me.") Mrs. Wolfgang tells Tilly, "Go on ahead then." Tilly jumps up and states very matter of fact, " Creatureville was founded by our Mayor's Grandfather Frankenstein's Monster in the year 1862, exactly 150 years ago."
" Very good Tilly, that is correct. Now please sit down,"

replies the teacher. " Since it's almost founder's day, I thought I would tell you about the finding of our little town. There was an extremely brilliant scientist among the humans, who's knowledge was way before his time. He was a genus and maybe a bit eccentric. This great man wanted to create life by building his own creature out of dead human parts. So Doctor Frankenstein and his assistant Igor proceeded to collect dead human specimens. Doctor Frankenstein skillfully put the cad-avers together until he created his masterpiece. The amount of electricity that was required to bring the creature to life was so enormous, that he knew only lighting would have the voltage that was required. Igor mounted lightning rods on the roof of the castle with wires leading to their newly built man. They installed bolts into the creature's neck so they would conduct better. On a very stormy night, with a high velocity of lightning, Doctor Frankenstein put his plan to work. Lightning struck the rods, electricity traveled down the wires into the body of the creature. Lo and behold he came to life. Doctor Frankenstein had created life. His creature was alive, he lives, he lives.

 Unfortunately the humans of the small village nearby were very ignorant and superstitious. Doctor Frankenstein would have to keep his creature a secret until he could teach and train the new being.
The creature was like a small child and would have to be taught everything. Igor helped the doctor work with the large man, while at the same time they built a companion for him. As soon as she was built , with the aid of lighting

21

again, the doctor,s new creature was brought to life. The good Doctor tried to keep his creatures a secret until the world would be ready to see his new beings. But somehow the villagers found out what Doctor Frankenstein had done. They stormed the castle and killed Doctor Frankenstein and chased after the monsters and Igor with pitch forks and torches blazing with fire. The villagers set the large castle on fire as they screamed and cursed the creature and yelled for their deaths.

Igor managed to lead the two beings down into a dungeon deep in the depths of the Earth. Like all castles there were hidden corridors and secret passageways. In the back of the dungeons was a cave that led them out of the large castle. But only into more danger. It is told there are many horrors in the caves they passed through trying to get to safety. After surviving the cave and all of its secrets, they found themselves in a very dark dense forest with animals and insects like no one had ever seen. (The bell rings.) OK class, make sure you start reading chapter 13 for the test tomorrow. Class dismissed."

Finally lunch time, Warren and Ernie run to their lockers and grab their lunches. As fast as they can, they run to the lunch area outside. Ernie is a short round boy with dark rim glasses that resemble the bottom of soda pop bottles, bottoms. His short black curly hair lays snug to his scalp. "Well Ernie it looks like we get the table by the dumpsters again," Warren says with a disgusted look on his face.
" Yea, well one of these days we will be upstairs and rule

the school. Then we won't have to eat by the smelly dumpsters," exclaims Ernie with a bit of a smile on his face.

The pair sit down going through their brown paper bags swapping their food and start to eat their lunch.
"Hey look there's loser and loser-er, HA!HA!HA!HA! HA!" Roland and his friends say while laughing at the pair of younger boys.
"Cut it out or I am going to tell Maw!" yells Warren.
"Boohoo, poor little baby, being picked on." says Roland in a whiny voice.

"Go away and leave us alone," Warren says angrily at his older brother. Roland and his friends walk off laughing and pretending to cry, making fun of Warren.
"I'm so tired of my bigger brothers picking on me all the time. One of these days I'm going to show them all. You watch and see." exclaimed Warren.
"Boy am I glad I'm the only child. No one around to pick on me. What do you want to do after school today?" asks Ernie.

" Will you go to Pumpkin Meadows with me and help me practice my flying?" asks Warren. "Pop won't buy me a new broom until I get better on my old one. Besides I want to win the broom race on Monday. First prize is a brand new state of the art broom."
"Sure Warren, I'll have to stop at my house to let my Mom know. We can meet at the bridge if you want." answers Ernie. (Bell rings.)

"Sounds great I'll meet you there." says Warren.

Warren makes it through the rest of the day without getting into too much trouble. His favorite two classes are Math and English, they make the day a little easier to take. But gym class is at the end of the day. They always play everyone's favorite game, Monster Walk. The gym teacher is Coach Wolfgang. Since Coach Wolfgang is the main coach for Monster Walk he always plays practice rounds for the game looking for potential players for the varsity games. Warren and Ernie are not very good at it, they always get picked last, then get yelled at and blamed when their team loses. In the gym is a small practice field for the game that's always set up. There are half as many tombstones as the real Monster Walk field, with a small make shift porch to run the players up and over. The object of the game is to scare humans through the make shift cemetery, through an old house, to the gate at the other end of a cemetery. While at the same time, keep your opponents from doing the same thing. In the gym, fake wooden tombstones are used, the monsters don't get as dressed up as they would in a real game. This is for practice only.

The two best players are used for the captains, who are Morris Mummy and Darmus Dracula. They take turns picking team members. As it gets down to the last of the players, Morris notices there is one too many kids. Darmus says,"Go ahead, you can have both Warren and Igor, it'll take both of them to make up for one player anyway." everyone laughs.

A short game is played for practice, so points are not given. The main thing is to get the humans to scream and through to the other side. Witch Hazel is on site to conjure up the teenagers for the game. Don't worry, when the teenagers get through the gate, they go back to sleep in their beds thinking they just had a nightmare. The lights are turned down low, with some fake fog for effect, a scream is made to start the game. This startles the teenagers so they start to move through the tombstones. Warren pops up to try and scare one of the girl teenagers. All the girl did is turn around and laugh at him, the gym roars with laughter. One of the monsters on Warren's team ran up behind her and scares her, up through their side of the makeshift graveyard. The other team intercepted the girl and ran her back through. Ernie tries to jump out in front of the girl to scare her but she totally ignores him, running right past him as if he didn't exist. Meanwhile the other team is running their teenager through the course, right past Warren and out the gate on Warren's team side. The girl teenager is scared through Warren's gate also. The other team won, they start shouting and yelling. While Ernie's and Warren's team members yell at them for making them lose the game.

Chapter 3
Trouble in Green Swamp

Warren and Ernie meet at the bridge as planned, then they run off to the open field for flying practice. Warren said, "let's go way over there where no one can see us".

"Not too far back there, it's awful close to the Green Swamp." Ernie replies, as the two boys walk toward the back of the large pumpkin patch.

When they get to what they think is a good place, Ernie holds onto Warren's broom while Warren climbs on it."Hold it still" Warren says, his broom always seems to have a mind of its own. ZOOOOOOM! Warren and his broom take off in a flash. Ernie jumps on his magic carpet and tries to catch up with him.

Ernie has always been as round as he is tall. As a small child it was difficult for him to walk and keep up with his friends. So his parents got him a small magic carpet to help him. It's not very fast and it's very small. But Ernie still uses it and when he sits on it he covers the entire carpet so all you can see are the tassels hanging down. Ernie can see Warren lose control of his broom. All of a sudden Warren is sent head over heals into the Green Swamp. Ernie finally gets up to the area where it looked like Warren went in. He stands on the edge of the swamp and yells for Warren. No answer, so Ernie edges into the swamp a little more and yells Warren's name again and asks if he is alright. Still no answer. This time he goes in deeper into the wicked swamp while yelling Warren's name.

"Warren! Are you alright, answer me, Warren, War...." Suddenly someone puts their hand around his mouth and pulls Ernie off of his carpet and onto the ground.
"Shh" Warren says with his finger at his mouth making a quiet sound. "look over there, what does that look like to you?" There in the dark and mist of the scary swamp they can see two figures. One being is very tall with large broad shoulders and long hairy arms. The other is very small about their size. The two boys continue to stare trying to make out what the figures are. Suddenly the two figures disappear into the murky water. They hardly move the water at all as they dive into it.
"What do you think that was?" Ernie whispers to Warren.
"I...I don't know....it looked like some kind of bear. But they walked upright more like us. We better get out of here before they come back and see us." replied Warren.
"Let's go!"
The two boys get up on their feet and run as fast as they can out of the creepy swamp. Ernie's carpet following behind them. They did not stop running until they got up by where the wild pumpkin patch starts. The two boys each sit on a large pumpkin trying to catch their breath.
"Whew, that was scary, let's never do that again," pants Ernie.
"We may have to," Warren replies.

"WHAT DO YOU MEAN!" exclaims Ernie.

"My broom is still in there, we have to get it back. Pop won't buy me a new one just because I lost my old broom. He will say if I can't take better care of what I have there is no sense in getting another one." Warren says with a sad look on his face.

"Look you're not that good at flying anyway, why don't you just give up on it," says Ernie wanting to find a way to talk his friend out of going back into the black forest to get his broom.

"No! I want to fly more than anything. Besides how can I win the race on Monday without my broom or some way to fly." Warren says trying not to cry in front of his friend.

"OK, OK, but its getting late and if I am not home in time for dinner, I'll be grounded for a week. We'll try again tomorrow after school to see if we can find it. Hey, maybe Witch Hazel or Harry can tell us where it is." replies Ernie trying to make his friend feel better.

"Great Idea! Let's go to her house after school tomorrow and ask her," says Warren with a little smile on his face. Warren enters the crooked stone tower that the Frankenstein's have called home since it was built by Warrens great grandfather. It was the first building ever built in the area and was used for a lookout tower. There was a great fear of villagers finding them to attack and kill the monsters. The inside of the tall tower is very simple and plain. As you walk into the house there is a small living room area with a fireplace, a long couch, two chairs and an old TV. You can see the rickety stairs with a hand railing made out of twisted tree limbs. The stairs run along the outside wall curving its way up the tower with a landing area at each doorway before it continues up to the very top door. Where the old lookout room was, that is where Warren's room is now. On the main floor in the back of the tower is a dining room with an extension that was added on by Warrens grandfather as a kitchen area. The dining room table is just big enough for the family of five, or should I say six, including Ernie.

Warren just made it home in time for dinner himself, he quickly washes his hands and sits at the table.
"Where have you been today?" asks his Mother.
"I was practicing flying my broom with Ernie."
"Why don't you give that up, you can't even ride a bicycle. How are you ever going to be able to fly a broom?" his oldest brother Frankster asks.
"Warren I talked to Professor Madly today. He said you are having trouble in his potion class again. Why don't you consider taking other classes next year. You struggle so in all of the magic prep classes. I'm not sure that magic is for you. Besides its affecting your grades so much. Even with all of the extra credit it still may not get you through to the next grade." says Maw.

"You wait and see, I'm going to be a great warlock someday. I know I can do it. Witch Hazel says she can see the potential in me." Cried Warren as he jumps up from the table and stomps his foot. With tears in his eyes he ran up the stairs to his room slamming the door behind him.

Warren shares this room with his older brother Roland. It's a lot like the rest of the house. There is a set of homemade bunk beds, made out of small trees with the bark still on them. The room includes two small wooden dressers, a desk and chair. A tall window that separates the dressers with a window seat. The window has a latch on it and opens like a door, so you can go out and walk around the balcony that encircles the high tower. From here Warren can see Ernie's house. They like to signal each other with flashlights. Warren sits at the desk to start his home work, saying to himself, "Wait and see. I'll show them, I'll show them all."

Chapter 4

Witch Hazel and Harry

After school the next day Warren and Ernie meet at the bridge again. They discuss all the options that they have. The only thing they feel they can do is to talk to Witch Hazel. Witch Hazel lives in a Victorian style house on the edge of town. The house has a large circular front porch that runs from where the living room extends out, and down the side of the big house to the back door. There is a lot of fancy gingerbread decorating the large porch. It's a very large two story house painted purple with green and yellow trim. She is an adviser and a tutor for most of the young witches and warlocks of the small town. A lot of the older creatures tend to stay away from her. She can be a bit eccentric, and will say just exactly what is on her mind. Her wild looking hair is a salt and pepper color with dark purple streaks running through it. Her pet or companion is a very large black hairy spider named Harry. Harry talks to Witch Hazel only and he can predict the future or find things that are lost.

The two boys ring her doorbell. "Why hello boys, I've been expecting you. Come in, come on in and sit down over here," The old witch says holding her hand out pointing toward the large front room. The boys smile a little nervous smile, and do as they are told. In front of them are two glasses of pumpkin punch and cookies. Witch Hazel continues as she sits down,"Help yourselves boys, I made them just for you. So Warren you've lost

31

your broom in the swamp."

"Y-Yes Ma-am," stammered Warren.

"Well my dear boy if you want to find something you need to want it. I sense you really don't want your broom back," says Witch Hazel.

"It's not that I don't want it. I'm having a hard time learning how to fly on that old thing. It's so awkward and slow, the training brooms seem to get in the way. I think I can learn better on a new, faster broom. Mr. Troll has all of those new brooms at his shop. They are all so shiny and new and look like they could go faster than anyone else around." replies Warren.

"So you think new is better. The only reason you're having trouble on your starter broom is because you have given up before you have even started." answers Witch Hazel. You must believe that you can fly before it will happen. Believe me my dear boy, believe, or all of the practice in the world will not help you," lectures the old witch.

"It doesn't matter now, I lost it in Green Swamp. Nothing has ever been found once it has been lost in there," whines Warren.

"Have you ever heard the story of how I lost my broom. It was destroyed by humans, long ago when I lived in a town called Salem. They were killing and destroying anyone who they thought was a witch. Most of the women that were killed were not witches. I tried to hide the fact that I am a witch, but somehow the humans found out. One day while I was away in the woods looking for needed roots and herbs for one of my potions, they came. I always kept my wonderful broom hidden in a secret panel in the back of a cupboard. As I neared my small cottage I could hear my dear sweet broom screaming. The humans were standing around my house yelling die witch die, while watching my house burn to the ground. They must of thought that my broom was me. Fortunately I was able to hide from the angry mob in the woods. My poor dear broom, there was nothing that I could do but run for my very life. I wandered around aimlessly for years, afraid to settle down again. That was until I found this haven for us monsters that your great grandfather was able to create. He started a wonderful community for the creatures of the world. You must always cherish your broom. It can be the best companion you will ever know. It may even save your life one day as mine did." Witch Hazel says with a sorrow filled voice.

The two boys just look at each other. They feel bad for the old woman. How could anyone be so cruel as to burn down a house with someone screaming inside.

"Now let's see what Harry has to say on the subject. Harry come out come out wherever you are," The witch sings out to her large pet. Harry comes running out of a closet by the front door. The big furry spider rubs it's legs together and climbs up onto Witch Hazel's shoulder and whispers into her ear."Harry wants me to tell you the story about how we met. I found Harry as a baby spider. He was no bigger than a gnat. The tiny thing was struggling trying to make a web. He could not weave his web at all. Harry had such a hard time trying to make his string work. He would have starved to death if I had not taken him in and fed him. Harry would get so frustrated when he would try to make a web, but to no avail he just could not do it. He wanted to give up so many times. But I urged him just to believe in himself, that he could do anything he set his mind to. Finally after telling himself over and over again, that he could do it. He made a beautiful web. The prettiest web I have ever seen. Now Harry can take care of himself, I no longer worry about him being able to feed himself," says Witch Hazel.

Harry whispers in her ear again. Witch Hazel turns and smiles at the boys and informs them, "Harry says that your broom has moved. For now it is in the northern part of green swamp. Harry will make you a map. Come back in the morning to get the map. Then you will need to be off immediately."

"B-But that will take us almost two days to walk there." stammered Warren.
"Yes it will, but only a short flight back, once you have retrieved your broom," replied Witch Hazel.

"OK, we will be back in the morning, goodbye and thank you for your help," the two boys say on their way out the door.

As the boys walk back toward town Warren says to Ernie, "We could tell our parents that we will be staying at each others house. That we will be camping in each others back yard. Do you think your parents will let you?"

"Maybe they will if they think I'll be at your house. That's a great idea. We'll need our camping gear for a trip like that," replies Ernie.

"Great, you run home and ask your parents, I'll run home and ask mine if I can camp in your back yard," Warren says excitedly, as they each start to run, or Warren runs while Ernie flies, towards their homes. They wave at each other when they come to the light in town and turn to head for their houses.

Chapter 5
Camping Out

Thank goodness it's Friday, that means Roland and Frankster are off with their friends doing whatever teen creatures do. At dinner, Warren asks his parents in a whiny voice, " Ernie and I want to go camping in his back yard tomorrow night, so we can spend more time in Pumpkin Meadows to practice flying. Can we pleeeeease?"

"Did Ernie's parents say it was OK with them? You know the carnival starts tomorrow morning" answers his father. "Yea, but we want to go camping so we can spend more time in the meadow so I can practice flying. Besides the carnival will still be open all three days of the festival. I really need all the practice I can get to be able to fly in the broom race on Monday," whines Warren.

"Mother how does that sound to you?" Pop Frankenstein asks his wife as he turns to look at her.
"Let's let them do it. It's a special weekend, they're old enough to make some decisions on their own. Why don't you go ahead and spend the night in the meadow. We know where you'll be." answers Maw.

"Thank you, thank you!" Warren says excitedly as he jumps up and gives both of his parents a kiss on the cheek and a hug. He runs to the phone to call Ernie, and tells him the great news. Ernie's news is just as good, his parents said it would be alright for Ernie to camp at the

Frankenstein's.

Warren is so excited he can hardly sleep all night. He gets up early before anyone else does. Warren packs several sandwiches in his backpack for their trip. He makes sure they have matches and snacks. Warren runs outside to see Ernie on his magic carpet flying up the drive. Ernie shows Warren his new compass that his parents gave him for their birthday. "Good idea," Warren says as he slaps his friend on the back. The two boys run into the garage to find Warren's old red wagon. They put a small pup tent and some of the other camping gear that will be too heavy to carry, into the red wagon. Also some extra water in old milk jugs. They each fill up canteens and put them over their shoulder. Finally they are ready and head towards Witch Hazel's to get the map that Harry had promised them.

As they walk through town they see all of the carnival rides and games that were set up overnight. Some men are still working on some of the rides checking them out. The two boys wave at the men working before they stop at "J.R. Troll's New and Used Brooms and Transportation". Warren stops and peers in the window at the "Newest Broom Sensation of the New Millennium", the sign reads. The Majestic IV.
"Doesn't that broom look wonderful. Its long and sleek with deep black lacquer finish and dark purple broom bristles. The dark purple pin-stripes down each side of the broomstick makes it look even faster. Can you see me flying that broom everywhere. Streaking through the sky with such grace and ease. I bet everyone would applaud

me as I go by, instead of laughing at me." Warren says as he pushes his nose against the big glass window.

"Hello boys," happily exclaims Mr. Troll. J.R. Troll is Tilly's father. You can tell, he has green skin, pointy ears and bright yellow eyes just like hers. He is more round through the middle though. Mr Troll tries to make it look like he has hair on top of his bald head by combing the hair from one side of his head over it. He also sports a pencil thin mustache. The man talks as fast as an auctioneer, he also talks non stop. It's a wonder he can ever catch his breath. "Warren are you ready for that new broom yet? Aah, I see you are looking at the latest thing in broom transportation. It's considered the absolute newest broom sensation of this millennium. It's wild and sleek and will take you places that normally you could only dream about. Have your Father come and see me, I'll make him a deal he just can't refuse. I have a great deal, just for him. I know you're ready to upgrade to a new broom. Got to run boys, time to open up. Don't forget to have Pop come in and see me. Bye" J.R says. He disappears into the store just as fast as he appeared. The boys can be see him inside the store hurrying around. "Boy I wonder with him and Tilly living in the same house, if anyone else gets a chance to talk at all?" Warren asks Ernie. Both boys turn and look at each other and start laughing. They laugh all of the way to Witch Hazel's house.

Warren reaches up and pushes the door bell on the witches front door. The door opens with a loud squeal,

Witch Hazel calls from inside the house,"Come on in boys, come on in. How are you two young lads doing this fine morning? Harry scurried over to the boys with the map in his mouth, as Witch Hazel explains, "Here is your map as promised. Follow the directions exactly and you will find your broom. The starting point is at the center of town under the traffic light. The place for you to camp tonight is indicated on the map. Make sure you camp there tonight or you will not get to your broom on time. For it seems to be in the hands of something else." Warren's and Ernie's eyes pop wide open and simultaneously exclaims, "What!"
"Now hurry along boys if you want to find that broom. Remember Warren if you want to be able to fly you must really want it." Witch Hazel bids them goodbye as they go out the door. The two boys look back over their shoulders as they head out the door and off of the porch.

They walk to the center of town to the traffic light and open up the map to look at it.

"OK, it says here we head straight north until we find a golden rain tree," Warren reads aloud. Ernie gets his compass out, opens it and they watch the needle shake back and forth until it points north. They start walking in the direction the compass indicates.

"What's a Golden Rain Tree, and what did she mean that the broom is in the hands of something else?" Ernie asks. "I don't know but I'm sure we'll find out when we get there" answers Warren.

"That's what I'm afraid of" replies Ernie.

The boys walk straight north as instructed by the map for a couple of hours, before Ernie says "lets stop and take a break."

"I don't know if we have time." replies Warren.

"Oh just a couple of minutes, my feet hurt. Look, there's some rocks just up ahead we can sit on" begs Ernie.

"OK, OK, just a couple of minutes though. We still have a very long way to go" answers Warren.

"How about a drink of water?" asks Ernie.

"Sure, sure I guess I do need some. I wonder what Witch Hazel meant by I really have to want it? Of course I want my broom, so I can get a new one. But I have to learn how to fly my old broom before I can get a new broom. Of course I want it." says Warren with a puzzled look on his face.

"Maybe you don't want your old broom for the right reasons" says Ernie.

"Let's get going Ernie we still have to find that tree. If it helps why don't you ride your carpet for a while, I'll pull the wagon" says Warren.

Warren takes another look at the map and says, "look I think these are the rocks we were sitting on, they have appeared on the map. I... wonder what the wave marks on the paper mean. They are between us and the tree." Ernie looks over his shoulder at the map and says, "Wow, you're right Warren it does look like the rocks. I didn't notice that before, or the wave marks. Let's get going, I feel rested now.

As the two young boys walk along they start to sing some of their favorite songs, "Let's do the mash, the monster mash, let's do the mash, it was a graveyard smash,"
"I think I know what those wave marks mean on the map. Look, it's a river. How are we going to get across that?" Ernie exclaims.

"I don't know, I didn't even know a river was here. Let's get closer, maybe we can find a way across." answers Warren.
They walk down to the river bank and look around. Warren takes his backpack and his shoes off. He sets them down on the river bank and proceeds to wade in.
"This seems to be really shallow, I wonder if we can walk across" says Warren.

"Be careful," Ernie warns. As soon as that is said Warren suddenly goes under the water completely out of site.
"WARREN! WARREN!" yells Ernie running up to the waters edge.
Gasping for breath Warren pops up out of the dark water. Paddling and splashing Warren finally gets on the shallow ground.
"I guess there's a drop off there." Warren says gasping for his breath.
"Very funny," Ernie says sarcastically.
"Hey look I didn't see that before, its a row boat. I wonder who that belongs to. There doesn't seem to be any houses, or anyone around." Warren says as he looks around. "It looks big enough to carry us and all of our

stuff."

"Wow, you're right." answers Ernie.

Warren wades over to the boat and grabs the rope on the front of the boat. He pulls it over to where Ernie and their things are. They load up the small rowboat with everything including the wagon. The boys carefully get into the boat. Warrens takes the oars and rows out onto the mysterious river.

Ernie looks at the map again and notices, "Hey we're not suppose to cross here but go down the river to a dirt landing with a tree on each side of it."

"What, let me see that. All of that was not on the map before." says Warren scratching his head.

"This map keeps adding stuff as we go along. I should have known if Witch Hazel and Harry had something to do with it. OK that's what we'll do then." Warren continues, "Let's look for that landing down river. I hope we find it soon, I want to get out of these wet clothes."

The boys are a little quieter this time waiting for some new thing to befall them. They allow the current to move them down the river only using the paddles to guide them. They point out the wild life to each other as they pass, a small deer, a couple of field mice. Some birds fly over head.

"It's so quiet and peaceful here. I could float along here forever," Ernie says softly.

Suddenly they hear a roaring sound, and the water is

moving faster.

"What...what's that noise!" Ernie yells.

"I...I don't know but let's get to shore." Warren yells back over the noise of the river.

Warren grabs the paddles and starts working the boat towards shore.

Ernie yells, "look down there, it's the landing!"

"Yea, I think your right, let's head for it." Warren yells back.

Warren continues to work the paddles trying to get the boat to shore. The water seems to be fighting him. As he struggles, it takes all of his strength to manage the paddles and steer it towards the dirt landing. He works and steers and works the paddles some more. Somehow he manages to get to the area indicated by the map. Only just a couple of feet, before the water turns into some really rough and violent rapids.

"Wow that was close, how did you know how to do that?" Ernie asks.

"I don't know, but I'm tired. Let's rest here and have lunch. Do you mind getting the stuff out of the boat by yourself?" Warren asks.

"Sure, you rest, I'll get the stuff." Answers Ernie.

Ernie pulls the boat onto drier land and proceeds to get their red wagon out. It was turned upside down on top of everything. He gets each item out of the boat and loads them back into the wagon. When everything is put back in. Ernie pulls the wagon up to where Warren is sitting. He retrieves their canteens and a couple of sandwiches.

Gives one of each to Warren. Ernie sits next to Warren on an old fallen tree. Warren finally catches his breath and is starting to feel a little stronger. As the boys sit and eat their lunch the river suddenly swells up. Then it goes back down again just as fast as it came up. But the row boat is gone. As if to say OK you're done with it, the boat belongs to me. The two boys just stare at the river and back at each other, then shrug their shoulders.

The duo finishes their lunch so they start walking again. The boys walk for a couple more hours. Warren asks, "How much farther do we have to go?"
Ernie pulls the map out of his backpack, and looks at it intently.
"OK, we're suppose to continue straight north," replies Ernie.

Warren asks, "Straight over that small hill." Ernie nods his head as they start up the small hill. They walk for a short distance. "Something is wrong, the hill, it's getting higher and steeper." Both boys struggle with pulling the wagon and carrying their gear. They keep passing the wagon back and forth taking turns with the extra burden.

"Whew, what's going on here," Warren asks as the two boys collapse from exhaustion. "I'm beginning to wonder if learning how to fly is worth all this work. This hill didn't look this big when we started out. It's getting steeper and higher as we go," pants Warren, trying to catch his breath.

"Normally I would say let's give it up, but we've come too far now. It can't be much further to the rain tree. Besides the row boat is gone, how will we get back across the river," Ernie wheezes back.

"Yea, you're right. We've worked too hard to give up now, we must keep going. I want my broom so I can fly, flying is everything to me," Warren says with a new sense of commitment. The duo pick themselves up and start walking up the hill again. As they continue, the walk up the hill, it begins to get easier and easier. At last they reach the top.

As they look down the steep bank they can see the Golden Rain Tree at the bottom of the high hill.
"Let's look at the map again and see what we're suppose to do now," Ernie says.
"Look it shows two people riding a wagon down the hill," exclaims Warren! "Witch Hazel said to follow the map exactly, so lets get on the wagon and ride it down the hill," continues Warren. Both boys climb on the wagon and with a little shove of Warren,s foot off they go.

"Whee..." they both yell!
"Hey, I just thought of something; how are we going to stop?" Ernie yells the question.
"Look out, we're going to hit the treeee!" Ernie yells again. Both boys grab onto the sides of the wagon with their hands and squeeze their eyes shut waiting for the crash. Suddenly the wagon stops within inches of the

tree.

"Hey, that was great, let's do that again," Warren says while jumping off the wagon.

"No thanks, besides how could we ever get back up that hill," Ernie exclaims.

"OK, OK," replies Warren.

"Now what does the map say to do," Ernie asks?

"I didn't realize how hungry I am," says Ernie.

"Yea, I know what you mean, we have been so busy we didn't have time to think about our stomachs."

"Let's see, we're suppose to walk directly east of the golden rain tree and set up camp. Look, it shows a tent with a fire and everything," Warren answers. The youngsters go over to the beautiful rain tree and pull out their compass and walk directly east. They find stones in a round circle and know that this is where their campsite should be. They pitch their tent facing the way it shows on the map and collect some fallen branches for the fire. After the fire gets going they get out some sandwiches for their supper and a couple of snacks for dessert.

As the sun starts to set, they sing a couple of songs and get out some marshmallows to roast. The boys lay on their backs and count the stars. Of course a campout would not be the same without a farting contest. They laugh at each other, making fun of each others farts. Each boy tells a spooky story before they decide they are tired enough to sleep. As they crawl into their tent an owl hoots scaring them. They jump into their sleeping bags, cover themselves all the way up to their chins. Both youngsters barely say goodnight to each other, when they drop off to sleep.

The next morning the boys are up early. They feel rested and eager to start the day. Ernie and Warren gobble up their breakfast and quickly pack up everything. Another look at the map before starting out.

"Let's see.... The map shows to go back to the rain tree and head straight north from it. I hope this part of the trip is easier than yesterday was," Ernie says.
"Well don't count on it," replies Warren. They look at each other and laugh as they start walking due north.

Walking seems to be getting easier for the two boys. They find they do not need as many breaks or rest stops. "Look up ahead, there are some fallen logs there. Let's stop and have lunch, I'm getting hungry," Ernie says. "Sounds good to me. The sun is pretty high in the sky it must be about lunch time. I'm starving too." Warren replies.

As they sit and eat they notice that it is the last of their sandwiches and they only have a few snacks left. The boys pull out the map to examine it again and realize the entrance to the swamp is not far away.
 The map shows three different ways to get into the swamp.
"I wonder what this means? Which way should we go?" asks Warren.

"There is nothing blocking the entrance to the east or the west. The entrance straight ahead shows a grassy area and a long high fence with no gate. We'll have to try and climb that fence and get our stuff over it too." continues Warren. "Nothing is going to be easy on this quest."

"Let's try the west entrance first." answers Ernie.

The two boys walk west for a few yards, until they have gone past the grassy area. The ground is hard and rocky. They stumble over the rough ground and find it difficult to pull their wagon over it. At the edge of the rocky area, they find some dense thorny bushes that are impossible to get through.
"Well I guess we won't get through there. We need to turn around and try the eastern entrance I guess." says Warren.

They examine the map, now the rocks and bushes show on the map. But nothing is indicated at the eastern entrance. The boys turn around and walk back to the east, past the green grassy fenced in entrance. As they walk up to the eastern swamp entrance they can see that there is no grass at all and the ground is flat and dry. Just solid dirt and sand.
"Ernie you stay here and let me try to cross first. Somehow I just don't trust the looks of this." Warren tells his friend as he holds his hand up to Ernie to indicate stop.
Warren slowly walks out onto the dirt, it seems to be alright. He walks a little further, turns to tell his friend to

come on and all of a sudden Warren starts to sink.
"Run, Run," yells Ernie!
"I can't my feet are stuck in the mud," Warren yells back.
"I don't think that's mud, it's quick sand," yells Ernie.
"let me find something to get you out with, hold on."
Ernie looks around quickly and sees a long tree branch.
Warren yells, "Hurry, hurry I'm sinking!"

Ernie runs as fast as his short legs will carry him. He
grabs the branch, carries it back over to Warren. Ernie
walks out as far as he dares. He lays on his stomach and
holds the branch out to Warren.
"Grab hold," Ernie yells. With a lot of struggling, the
two boys manage to get Warren out of the quicksand.
"Whew, that was a close one. Maybe the straightest way
was the best, even though we have to climb over a
fence." Warren says.

The pair head back to the grassy area and start slowly
walking through the grassy field.
"So far so good," says Ernie.
"Let's walk a little faster just in case," Warren replies.
They pick up their pace and walk a little faster then faster
until they are running. They can now see a gate in the
fence. Ernie jumps on his carpet while Warren runs as
fast as he can.
As they reach the fence Warren exclaims,while trying to
catch his breath."There is a gate,(pant) I can't believe it!"
"But look it has a large lock on it." Ernie says pointing at
the lock.

"Quick look at the map and see what it shows. You know there is going to be more to this" Warren replies.

"It shows the gate open and us walking through it. But where is the key. There must be a key around here some place." says Ernie, as he looks around at the ground and along the fence.

But there is nothing in site or even any place to hide a key.

"What are we suppose to do now," whines Warren.

"Let's just try the lock to see if it is locked." replies Ernie as he walks over to the big gate and pulls on the lock.

"It's not locked! Talk about feeling dumb. I guess we should of checked first instead of just getting upset about it," Warren says as his face turns a little red.

The large gate opens up wide by itself as Ernie pulls the lock off. They gather up their things and go through the gate and find a narrow trail that will take them into the scary swamp.

"I wish we had gone straight and checked out the gate first. But you never know until you try," Warren says.

"Now comes the really scary part." As the two boys stand on the beginning of the trail and look up at the tall dark trees with the Spanish moss hanging all over them. They can hear strange squeals and noises inside the swamp. Which makes it seem even scarier.

"Let's check the map to be sure this is the right trail. I don't want to make anymore mistakes." Warren says. As they look at the map they can see everything that they have come across up to now and the trail with an arrow pointing into the large swamp.

"OK, let's do this," replies Ernie.

"From the looks of that trail I don't think we will be able to take the wagon with us. Let's leave it here. We'll be coming back this way anyway." Warren says.

"Yea you're right. Look, the map shows us leaving it behind." replies Ernie.

Chapter 6
The Green Swamp

Slowly step by step the two boys enter into the forbidden swamp. Both boys are afraid to speak or move very quickly as they continue to walk slowly further into the scary swamp. The path twists and turns around the tall trees. They have to push the hanging moss and vines out of their faces as they walk. As they continue deeper into the swamp, there are rustling sounds in the bushes. Ernie and Warren stop dead in their tracks and grab onto each other, too scared to move or say anything. The noise gets closer, it seems to be coming from behind them.

"Wh...What's that?" whispers Ernie.
"I...I don't know." answers Warren. As the two boys turn around they can see something in the path behind them. It walks closer to them, they can now see what it is. It's the biggest, meanest looking, wild boar they have ever seen. It has long huge tusks coming out of either side of his snout.

"Don't move or say anything, maybe it will go away," whispers Warren.
The pair stand frozen in their tracks clinging onto each other. Making sure not to move a muscle and just barely breathing. The large beast slowly inches towards them, it keeps moving closer and closer. When it gets within a couple of feet of the boys, it snorts at them, "follow me".

The boys turn and look at each other, scream and start

running up the path further into the swamp. They look behind them and realize that the boar is not following them so they stop to catch their breath.

"Did that thing say something or was that my imagination?" Ernie asks, while trying to catch his breath, leaning up against one of the old cypress trees.

"I thought I heard it say, 'follow me'," answers Warren. As he put his hands against another tree gasping for air.

"Yes I did, Please follow me boys," snorts the big beast, as he appears in front of them on the trail.

Both boys stand straight up and stare at the large beast, with a large GULP! They both shake their head yes and start to move slowly behind the beast. They keep looking at each other and wonder how they can escape from the wild boar.

The boar turns around looks at them and snorts, "Hurry up you don't want to get left behind. By the way my name is Beau." The two youngsters do as they are told and walk a little faster to keep up the large beast.

"My name is Warr..." Warren starts to say but is interrupted by Beau. "No need for names we have been expecting you."

"Wait, what about the map, we are suppose to do what the map says," Warren exclaims

"Look at your map," snorts Beau.

Warren pulls out the map and it shows them following a boar.

"You're right Beau, we are suppose to follow you," says

Warren.

The trio continues along the path until they come to a fork in the path. Beau leads them onto the northern trail without a second thought. As they walk along Beau snorts, "So you're Pop Frankenstein's son."

Warren looks a little shocked as he replies "Yes, you know my father?" Beau just nods his head and answers, "Yes, your father and I have done a little business in the past. Now keep up,we're almost there boys."

Soon they arrive at a clearing, with a lot of small mud huts around in a circle. There are several little piglets running around playing and laughing. A couple of large boars stick their heads out of some of the mud huts, while others stop what they are doing to look and stare at them. Beau snorts loudly, "This is young Frankenstein, go back to whatever you were doing."

One little piglet runs up to the boys wagging his little curly tail snorting, "Hi, I'm Junior. I'm so little cause I'm the runt of the litter. My dad says my mouth is to busy for someone so small. Will you be my friend? I like to have lots of friends. How old are you, you sure are big....."

"Junior, leave them alone and go and play with your siblings. We have a lot to get done. You will get to see them again." snorts big Beau.

Big Beau leads them through the little town, down a trail that heads in a northwest direction. They walk for about a half hour when Beau turns to them and snorts, "This is where I leave you boys. Don't look so worried, you'll be fine on your own." With that Beau scurries back up the trail.

"Are you sure you really want your broom? Maybe if we go back, we can tell your Pop how it was lost and that it wasn't your fault. He may feel bad and buy you a new one anyway." Ernie asks Warren.

"Yes, I want my broom, and you know he won't buy me a new one," answers Warren as he pulls out the map for further instructions. "According to this we continue on a little farther. Look, my broom is on the map just a little further up this path. Come on let's go, we're almost there." Warren says excitedly.

The pair walk on not sure what to expect next. They find a small clearing, they can see the broom.
"There it is, over there up against that tree!" Warren exclaims.

Ernie looks around at the trees and says, "do you feel like someone is watching us. I sure feel like there are eyes watching us." Warren ignores what Ernie had just said and runs for his broom. As he runs he does not pay any attention to the dark water he is running through.
"Finally..I got it...I got it!" exclaims Warren jumping up and down. Warren reaches for his broom, he manages to put his fingers on it. Snatch! the tree that it's leaning on, grabs it from him, using one of it's long thin branches.

The tree holds the broom up over Warren's head. Just out of his reach.

"Hey watch it there young fella, who do you think you are?" asks the extremely tall tree, with a deep booming voice. "This is my broom it's a part of me."
"W...What do you mean?" asks Warren with just a little studder from fear.
"This broom was once a part of me. One of my limbs was cut off of me to create this broom. See here where the scar is." growls the giant tree.

"I'm truly sorry Mr. Tree, but I was given that broom on my third birthday so I could learn how to fly. May I have it back please?" Warren says a little sheepishly.
"NO!" yells the large tree, as it makes the ground shake.
"It is said that you do not want the broom," continues the large tree.
Some of the other trees start chanting, "It's too small, it's too slow, it's too small, it's too slow."
"You must first prove to me that you are truly worthy to have this broom. That you will take better care of it from now on." grumbles the large tree.

"What do you want me to do?" asks Warren, sheepishly. The large tree instructs Warren, as he points. "You must dig up that sapling over there. It's rather sickly because it does not get enough sunlight. All of the larger trees block out the sun. We try to sway to give it light but it is just not enough. For, you see, it's my sapling and I want to make sure it'll be able to survive. I'm afraid it will not last much longer here. You must help me by saving my little sapling. Once you have transplanted it to my satisfaction, then I will let you have this broom back. I know all that goes on in the swamp, so be careful how you take care of my sapling. First you will need something in which to dig it up. Be careful not to lose to much dirt around its tender roots. Then wrap something around its tender roots to help keep the dirt and roots together to protect them. Next you will need to find a nice clearing where the little sapling can get plenty of sunlight and water. The earth must be rich and fertile. How you can tell, there must be plenty of grass and wild flowers. This is a sign of good fertile land. Now, are you sure you really want this broom?"

"Yes I'll do everything you ask," replies Warren.

Warren turns, looks at Ernie as he walks back across the shallow water to where Ernie is standing.

"Ernie, let's get out the map and see if it has any instructions as to what we should do next." Warren says to his friend.

Ernie just shakes his head as he opens up the map. "The map shows nothing more. I guess we are on our own now." informs Ernie. " Look, this is making me nervous. Do you really want to do this. We have already been through a lot because of your broom."

"Ernie if you do not want to go along that's fine. We can go back up to the Boar's village and maybe they will let you stay there until I get back. Whether or not I get my

Broom, I will try to help that little tree," says Warren. The two boys walk slowly up the path together going back to the Boar's Village. Warren hangs his head and whines, "What are we going to do now?"

"Let's think about it a minute. First we need to find a way to dig up the tree. Then put some kind of wrapping around its roots. Maybe Beau will help us." Ernie says as the boys smile at each other. Ernie jumps on his flying carpet while Warren starts to jog up the pathway.

They return to the Boar's Village and look around. But Beau is no where to be found. Little Junior runs up to the pair and starts asking questions, "Hi, how are you? Can you stay awhile? Will you play with me?"
"Yes to all," answers Warren. "We know a great game to play. Do you want to play?" Ernie looks at Warren with a puzzled look on his face. Warren just winks back at him. "Sure, yes, sure I want to play. The other piglets won't let me play with them. They say I'm too small." Says Junior while jumping up and down.

"OK, the talking trees have asked me to transplant a sapling. We need a way to dig up the little tree and also a way to cover its roots up once we get it out of the ground. They want us to find a better place for it to be planted. Do you think you can help us?" Warren informs the little pig.
"The older boar's use their tusks to dig down into the dirt looking for truffles. I don't have any tusks yet, so I use this piece of metal I found," answers Junior.

"Great, now all we need is something to put around its roots," says Warren.
Junior says, "Wait right here a minute." Junior runs off and disappears inside one of the mud huts. Warren and Ernie can hear some banging and thumping noises inside the hut. Shortly after the noises stop, Junior runs back out with something in his teeth.

"Here we can use this old flour sack to cover the roots with," says Junior as he drops the bag on the ground.
"OK, great let's go, I think we have everything we need," Warren replies.

Warren, Ernie and little Junior follow the path to where the giant talking trees reside. As they arrive at their destination Ernie says, "It still feels like we are being watched."
Warren replies, "That's just the trees watching us to make sure we don't hurt the sapling."
Ernie says, "No,no it's much more than that."

"Let's get busy and dig up the little tree. I want to get this tree moved before it gets too late." says Warren.
Warren and Ernie start digging up the tree, being careful not to harm it in any way. As they free the roots with as much dirt around the tender roots as they can, Junior gives them the bag so they can wrap it up warm and snug.

"Junior do you know of a place where we can move this tree to?" asks Warren.

"Sure, I know of a great place where there is plenty of sunshine, water and beautiful wild flowers that grow everywhere. This little tree would look beautiful there. Follow me, I'll take you there. It's not far, not far at all" answers Junior.

Ernie picks up the tree and places it in his back pack. He climbs onto his magic carpet and brings up the rear of the trio. As they pass the large talking trees, they all say together "Remember, take care of the little sapling." The boys all turn and wave saying "we will". Junior starts singing a song to help pass the time, soon they are all singing along.

They did not walk far when they came upon a large hill with a cave in the side of it.
"We have to go through this cave. It's the only way, or the shortest way, to get to where we are going. There is no way through all of those thorny bushes. To get around them it would take almost a half of a day. Since Boar's are such great diggers, we dug this cave so we could get to the wild flower clearing.
Ernie looks over at Warren and says, "If the boars use it all of the time, it can't be too bad. Let's go."

Junior leads his friends into the dark cave, finds a torch and lights it. The torch lights up the cave to reveal some steps that seem to wind and twist upward and around inside the cave.
Ernie with the sapling on his back, and Warren follow junior up the dirt packed stairs. It's very cold and damp.

Roots from the bushes hang down and tickle their faces from time to time. Once in a while, a worm will stick its head out and watch the boys as they continue up and around the twisting stairs.

"This tunnel sure has a lot of stairs, twists and turns. We have turned around in here so many times I have no idea which direction we're going. We keep going higher and higher. Are you sure this is the short cut Junior?" Warren asks as he scratches his head.

"Yes, just you wait and see. We'll be there in no time." replies Junior.
They continue to climb higher for a few more yards. Finally there are no more steps. Junior yells out. "Watch that last step and hold on, WHEEEeeeeeeee!!!"
"AUGHHHHhhhhh!!!!!" Warren yells as he falls and slides down a long dark muddy tunnel on his back. He slides faster and faster through the tunnel, as it twists and winds around and around in circles several times. All of a sudden Warren flies up over a ramp and into the air and sunlight. He flails his legs and arms in every direction trying to stop the flight. SPLASH! Into a small clear pond. "Wow that was great," Warren exclaims, while laughing, as he struggles to stand in the shallow water.

Junior and Warren can hear Ernie yelling "Help" all the way through the tunnel. When he flies out of the tunnel they can tell he has done a belly flopper all the way down. SPLASH! "Gasp! Gasp! Cough, you could warn a person about that ya know." Ernie says while choking and spitting water, as he tries to stand and get up out of the water.

"It's more fun if you don't know it's coming," says Junior, then they all laugh and vow to come back and do it again.

The trio walk a few feet when they come to the large clearing in the middle of the swamp. Junior is right, there are beautiful wild flowers growing everywhere with a babbling brook running through the middle of the clearing.

Warren suddenly remembers the tree. "How's the little tree? Is it all right?"Ernie takes his backpack off to look at it, "The tree seems to be fine, but my carpet sure is a mess. I may never get it clean again. Maybe I should just carry the tree for a while." He pulls the tree out of the pack carefully and cradles it in his hands.

"I think we should put the tree over there on that small hill by the stream. It's in the middle where it will get lots of sunshine and it will be able to get plenty of water from the brook." says Warren as he looks around at the beautiful site.

Warren pulls off his backpack and gets out Juniors little homemade shovel and starts digging. Junior helps as much as he can using his nose to dig. Soon the hole is big enough. They unwrap the roots carefully, while Ernie fills up their canteens to pour water around the roots. The dirt from the hole is put around the tree and packed around it so it will stand straight.

As Ernie pours he asks the little tree, "Is that enough water?"
"Oh yes, I feel so much better now." answers the little sapling.
"I...I didn't know that you could talk." says Ernie a little startled.
"Yes, but I was so sick and weak that I couldn't. I would like to thank you for saving my life. Thank you for finding me such a beautiful place to grow up in. Thank you so much. My father will repay you with your broom now. I am sure of it" says the little sapling, in a small quiet voice.

Warren says, "I hope you will get better here. But aren't you all alone now?"
"Do not worry, I have a lot of friends that will visit me often. You must come back and see me again also. I would like that very much." replied the little tree. It stretched its tiny branches out as far as it could to let the sunshine on its leaves. You can tell it's getting stronger already. You can hear the tiny tree take a deep breath in and then let it out.

"We need to go little tree. Best of luck to you. Good Bye." Warren says with a big smile on his face, as he turns and waves at the tiny tree.
"Good Bye to you and please do come again," responds the little tree as he waves at his new friends.
They all wave at the tiny tree, very proud of themselves

for helping it.

"Let's go back. Ernie and I need to get back to Creatureville. It's getting awfully late. Our parents will be wondering where we are. Which way do we go Junior."
"Well....I'm not real sure how to get back from here." Junior replies as he lowers his head and scrapes the dirt with his front hoof.

"What! What are we going to do now? How are we going to get back?" Warren exclaims.
"Sorry, I'm usually tired so my Dad carries me on his back, and I always fall asleep. So I never see which way we go." answers Junior feeling bad for getting them lost.
"But, I know the trail starts over there by that big weeping willow. I'm sure of that."
"Let's look at the map maybe it will help us. Warren, I think it's in your backpack. Look and see." Ernie says while pointing to Warren's backpack laying on the ground.

Ernie keeps looking around and says in kind of a whisper, "I'm getting that "someone is watching us" feeling again."
"You're just paranoid," replies Warren, as he picks up his pack and rummages through it. He finally finds the map, but it's all wet and muddy from the slide on the hill. Warren tries to carefully open it, but it's made of paper and it falls apart.

"Oh no, now what are we going to do? We can't get back up that slide, or can we?" asks Ernie.

"Well we will have to find our way ourselves. Do you still have your compass?" Ernie searches for his compass and exclaims, "I can't find it, it's gone."

Junior says "The trail starts over there, by that weeping willow tree. I'm sure of it.

"Let's get started Junior, lead the way please." says Warren trying to make the little piglet feel better about getting them lost.

The young creatures start down the path with the little piglet leading the way. Ernie keeps looking around at all the trees and tries to see into the brush. He gets more and more nervous the deeper they go into the black woods. Finally in a squeaky voice he says "I am telling you we are being watched. I know these trees don't talk so it's not them."

Warren looks at his friend and asks, "Are you sure?"

"Yes," replies Ernie, still looking around at all of the trees. "Hey Junior, do you know of anything that would be watching us?"

"No," answers Little Junior, "Unless it's...it's, no that can't be. Those tales aren't true. They are only bedtime stories."

"What are you talking about Junior?" Warren asks.

"Well there is a big hairy creature that lives in the woods. No one ever gets a good look at it. Or all anyone finds are giant foot prints that look kind of like a humans." answers Junior.

"What's this creature called?" asks Ernie.

"Bigfoot," answers Junior.

"Bigfoot," echos Warren and Ernie.

"Is it dangerous, will it hurt us?" asks Ernie.

"Well... I don't really know, cause no one ever gets near it. I'm not sure if it's animal, human, creature, or what." answers Junior.

The boys keep walking along looking in every direction wondering if this thing is going to jump out and get them. Before you know it the path has disappeared, they have come to a dead end. There are bushes and scrubs all around them with no visible way out.

"OK Junior now what do we do?" asks Warren.

"I... don't know." answers Junior almost in tears.

"What?" exclaims Ernie, as his eyes almost pop out of his head.

"Let's all calm down and think a minute." says Warren. There's a rustling sound in the bushes behind them. The trio turns around and jumps all at the same time. They see the bushes move and they freeze right where they are. A rabbit runs out from behind a bush. With a sigh of re-leaf, they all relax.

"Let's look behind that bush to see if there might be a path behind it." Warren says.

"OK" replies Ernie and Junior. But before any of them could move, out from behind a tree steps a 10 foot giant hairy monster looking creature. The three boys all hold onto each other and shake.

"Hello there young fellows, where are you going?" asks the hairy giant.

"We... need to go to the talking trees and get my broom back. We replanted a sapling for the talking trees." answers Warren shakily.

"I know a short cut and can get you there quickly. By the way my name is Larry and this is my son Carry." replies Bigfoot. Out from behind another tree comes a little hairy creature about the size of Warren and Ernie.

"Sorry if I scared you, I watch out for all living things in the forest. My job is to make sure no one is here to harm any living thing in the swamp. Normally I do not show myself but you boys look like you need help." continues Larry.

"Thank you so much, we are lost and really need to get back home soon. Our parents will worry." replies Warren.

As Larry Bigfoot leads the group back to the parent tree, all of the young creatures talk and jabber getting to know one another. Little Junior starts getting tired so Larry picks him up and carries the small piglet the rest of the way.

Warren asks, "Why don't you move to Creatureville? You would be more than welcome there. It would be great to be able to play with Carry more."

Larry replies, "No, my job is here in the forest, we are very happy here. This is our home. But maybe we can come and visit. It would be nice if you came back to visit also. This is where we must leave you. Go through that clump of trees and you will be back at the talking trees.

"Come to the Founder's Day Festival and join in some of the games and fun. Carry can ride on the carnival rides with us. Junior, let's ask your dad if you can come too. It would be more fun if both of you were there." Warren says.

They all say their goodbyes before walking away from each other. Each group turns and waves one more time before they disappear into the dense woods.

It's just a short walk through some trees when Warren realizes they are standing in front of the giant talking trees. The little sapling parent tree is so happy that his little one is doing so well in the clearing they found just for him. The tree gives Warren his broom back and makes him promise to take better care of it. Warren agrees readily and now knows how important it is to do so. Warren and Ernie thank the trees and head back up the trail to the Boar's Village.

When they reach the small village they are greeted by some of the other piglets and their parents wanting to know about their adventure. Warren and Ernie tell them that Junior would have to tell them all about it. They ask Junior's father about the Founder's Day celebration. Beau said that he would think about it. They all say goodbye. Warren and Ernie turn to get back on the trail that leads out of the forest. Warren says, "Come on Ernie jump on, let's go home."

"You couldn't fly that thing by yourself, now you want me to get on it with you?" Ernie says.
"Jump on, I know I can fly it now, I know I can. You just wait and see I'm going to show everyone when we get back." Warren exclaims.
"It's getting late, how are we going to get back on time?" Ernie asks.
"Just get on, we will make it." replies Warren. Ernie reluctantly climbs onto the broom behind Warren.

Chapter 7
Monster Walk

Before they know it they are out of the Black Forest, but the wagon is gone. The boys stop and get off of the broom to look around. Warren pulls out what is left of the map. There is enough of it that shows his house.
"Don't tell me we are going to have to come back and get that stuff?" asks Ernie.
"No, look at the map, it's already back at my house." answers Warren.

"What are we waiting for, let's get going." Ernie says as he motions to Warren to get on the broom, Ernie jumps on behind him. Off they go across the meadows, past the golden Raintree, over the large hill and over the river, as if the broom has a mind of its own. They reach Warren's house in just a short time.

The boys make it home in time for supper. Bride invites Ernie to stay for dinner. The two boys eat as though they have not eaten in a week. Pop Frankenstein tells them to put away their gear after supper. Then they can all go to the Monster Walk Game. Frankster and Roland are playing tonight.

The object is to get the teenagers to walk or run through the gate at the opposite end of the field from where they came in at. Creatures chase and scare the teens through the seven rows of gravestones, through the house, upstairs and back down again. Then through the other seven rows of gravestones on the other side and out through the opposite gate or goal. While the other team is doing the same thing and trying to scare the opposite teams teenagers back through the gate at their goal. Referees flying on broomsticks keep track of the game and announce points, to be put on the scoreboard. There are two points for every teenager they get upstairs, and seven bonus points if the teenager faints. For each teenager that goes through the gate after being played at least once through the house gets thirteen points. The gate does not count if the teenagers does not go all the way through the house and touch the ground on the other side, before they are turned around. The game ends when all of the teenagers are through the gates.

The best way to play the game is in the dark with fog. There is an official field next to the school. It has a large two story house in the middle, with the outside walls gone so that everyone in the stands can see the inside of the house. There are bleachers on both sides of the field for the spectators. On Each end of the field are rows of tombstones to create a cemetery, with a cast iron gate at each end and a cast iron fence all around the make shift cemetery.

The teams that are playing tonight are the Howling Banshees versus the Screaming Ghouls. On the howling Banshee's team are Warren's brothers Frankster and

Roland, along with Manly Werewolf, Zack Dracula and Tilley's older sister Zinley Troll. You can't miss Zinley, she has really big hair that goes down to the back of her knees. It's bright orange with a streak of green running through it. She does have pointy ears but they are hard to see because of all of her hair. Her complexion is green just like her Fathers.

The Screaming Ghouls team consist of Morris Mummy (Doctor Mummy's son), Darmus Dracula, Henrietta Howard, Bob Wolfgang (Handy's Son) and Morty Mortuary (the son of Monty Mortuary, a tall thin creature with slicked back black hair, white skin and black bulging eyes. Who is made taller by his tall top hat that he always wears). The players dress out in their scariest gear and get into their positions on the field. The fog fills the field and Harry whispers into Witch Hazel's ear. Witch Hazel waves her hand and says some magic words to conjure up the three teenagers for each side of the field, a werewolf howls and the game begins.

The teenagers on both sides start moving into the graveyard. They get up past the first row of gravestones. Now the teens are approaching the second set of tombstones. This game seems to be starting kind of slow or is it a new strategy. All of a sudden a boy teen breaks away from the group (on the ghouls side). He runs up past the third row of tombstones and out jumps Henrietta, making him scream like a girl. He turns and runs sideways while the other two teens stand and grab each other screaming. All of a sudden Darmus flies up behind them as a bat and turns back into himself with his arm across in front of his face, with his cape draping over it so all that could be seen is his eerie red eyes. The two girls scream some more and start running towards the house, but they trip and fall. So the two girls hide behind row five of the gravestones. A great start for the ghouls.

While on the other side, one of the girl teens run ahead of the group as far as the fifth row of tombstones. Roland comes up from behind her walking with stiff legs, and his arms stretched out growling at her. The girl runs ahead to the sixth row of gravestones and hides behind one of them. Manly quietly walks up behind the other two teens that are standing between the second and the third row and howls. Which sends the pair running in opposite directions toward either side of the graveyard. It's an OK start but the Banshees need to get the teens to move closer to the house. Zinley flanks on the right side of the field and scares one of the teens into a faint. At last points on the scoreboard, that's seven points for the Howling Banshees.

Frankster moves towards the left side of the field and scares the teen enough so they run toward the house and catches up with the other teen in row six. They are both hiding behind the same tombstone when Zack Dracula flies up to them as a bat and buzzes around their heads. This makes the two teens jump up and run to the house and onto the porch. The spectators go wild, yelling and screaming. They all chant "the porch, the porch."

On the other end of the field the ghouls are moving their teens also. Up out of the ground Morris Mummy slowly gets up and starts walking towards the two girls in row five, making them scream and only run up one row to the far end of the playing field. Bob Wolfgang moves up behind them and howls scaring them enough so they run towards the house. Morris is able to chase them up to the seventh row. While Darmus and Henrietta are working on chasing the boy teen closer to the house also.

The Banshees are working on the two teens on the porch. Zack, as a bat, manages to chase them inside. The crowd really goes wild now, not one but two teens from one side are in the house. The teen that fainted on the right side of the field wakes up and slowly starts moving toward the house. He takes a few steps hides behind a tombstones, peers around it, then runs up to the next row and repeats what he had just done. Roland walks toward him doing the Monster Walk and growling. Which scares the teen all the way into the house, slamming the door behind him. This really puts the Banshees in a good position. But, be careful, it's still anyone's game.

The Screaming Ghouls are doing a great job of getting their teens onto the porch and into the house. Inside, Morty Mortuary takes over for his group slowly walking toward the teens trying to steer them toward the stairs for the extra upstairs points. He does manage to get one of the teens upstairs. Now the Banshees have two points on their side of the score board. Look, behind Morty, it seems that Darmus has managed to steer the other two teens up the stairs. The two monsters manage to chase the three teens around upstairs for a short time trying to get the teens down the other set of stairs that will lead them out the other side of the house. The crowd is going wild. What an intense game. The Ghouls have six points on the board, look out Banshees they are catching up to you.

Frankster manages to get one of their teens up the stairs, that was the only one that would go. This helps to keep their lead but the game could still be turned around. He managed to chase the teen through the upstairs and down the other flight of stairs toward the other side of the cemetery and toward the goal. The rest of the Banshees are getting themselves into place to set up for the Ghouls coming over to their side. Frankster scares the teen he has into row six and manages to keep him there. Zack is scaring the two girls through the house and out onto the porch on the other side.

The Screaming Ghouls finally have their teens downstairs and headed out the other door toward their goal. Morty and Bob decided to hang back to see if they can get one of the Banshee's teens. Morty gets one of the teens on the ground, Bob swoops in and scares the teen back into the house. Meanwhile Zack gets the teen he has over to Frankster who holds them in place.

Morty and Bob scare the stolen teen upstairs, through the house and out the other side before Zack can get around to the other side of the house. Zack tries to get his teams stolen teen back. Morty and Bob keep the teen and chases it all the way to the goal. The crowd screams with excitement over the first Gateway score of thirteen points. Once a teen is through the Gateway, they are out of play. The teens go back to their bed only to wake up thinking they had a nightmare. Now the Screaming Ghouls are in the lead with twenty-one points to nine.

The Howling Banshees have to really step up their game. With one lost teen they must steal one back. Frankster starts heading the two teens toward the Gateway. Manly runs up behind them scaring the two teens. Finally the teens start running, with the two monsters right on their heels, the teens run through the gateway as fast as they can. The crowd howls and yells at the double score.

Roland, Zack, and Zinley work on slowing up the other team. Frankster and Manly rush over to the other side of the house. Manly changes into a wolf, which helps them to steal two of the other team's teens. They chase the two teenagers through the house together, but they split up on the other side. Manly chases one down the outside of the makeshift gravestones on all fours. While at the same time, Frankster chases the other teen into row five of the gravestones.

Manly almost has his teen to row two when Darmus Dracula pops up and scares the teen all the way back to row six. Frankster finally gets his teen to move toward the Gateway. The teens start weaving in and out of the gravestones, through row four, three, two, one and finally out the iron gate. Frankster runs back to help his teammate. Together they get on each side of the teen to get him started back toward their goal. Manly tries to block again but the wolf manages to scare the teen past him and down through the headstones. The crowd howls and screams at the excitement of the game.

With one teen to go, the crowd starts chanting "Banshee's, Banshee's." The teen that fainted has been hiding in the house. Now everyone is trying to get the teen out of the house and onto their playing field. The Ghouls get the teen out of the house, but they are not aware of Frankster and Zack. Zack changes into a bat just as the teen runs out side onto the opposing team's porch. Zack scares him back inside and up the stairs through the house out the other side. Running as fast as he can the scared teen runs straight through the middle of the gravestones straight through the Gate. The Banshees win!

What a game, everyone screams and howls, except for the losing team. Everyone from the Banshee side of the bleachers run down and congratulate the game winners. Pop Frankenstein pats his sons on the back and offers to take the entire team to Zombie Hut for a late night treat. There is nothing like a pumpkin swirly and sweet potato fries after a great game.

Chapter 8
Broom Race

What a great way to start Founder's Day, with an exciting game of Monster Mash. Everyone was talking about it the next morning at the Founder's Day Celebration. Of course this is the biggest event of the year. Everything closes including the school and stores. You can hear people laughing and talking everywhere. The small carnival that comes every year manages to set everything up overnight. The Ferris Wheel is already busy with customers on it. There is also a swing ride that goes around in a circle, the faster it goes the farther out the swings go. You can hear the bumper cars crashing and the Tilt-A-Whirl's music is playing really loud, that means its going really fast.
Look at that cute little train for the smaller kids, and the little airplanes that just go around in a circle. Of course, it would not be a carnival without the merry-go-round.

In the midway are all types of games from throwing darts at balloons, to fishing for plastic ducks out of a small pond. Of course, the Mrs. Monster's Auxiliary have a cake walk and a bazaar to raise funds for whatever project they decide is needed. There will be a pumpkin contest for the best home grown pumpkin, as well as the broom race and the talent contest later in the day.

Warren hurries over to the bandstand at the park so he can sign up for the Broom Race. It is more of an obstacle course that test the riders ability as well as their speed. Normally kids as young as Warren do not sign up for it. You must be an above average broom rider. Mr Troll is an official for the race, he asks Warren, "Are you sure you want to sign up for the race young man? You know there are going to be a lot of experienced fliers this year. Plus it is a very tough course."

"Yes, I know, Mr. Troll, but I know I can do it." answers Warren.

"OK, here ya go," replies Mr Troll as he hands Warren his number and his placement position.

Warren runs all the way to Ernie's house to get him.

"Hello Mrs. Igor, can Ernie go to the festival with me."

"Sure" Mrs. Igor barely gets out of her mouth when Ernie comes bounding outside to greet his friend.

"Bye Mom see ya later."

They say opposites attract: that's for sure in the case of Ernie's parents. His Father is short and round with a hump on his back, bald headed with dark rings around his eyes. While his Mother is very tall, thin, almost like a skeleton with long white hair that touches the floor.

Ernie turns to Warren and asks, "Hey, how are you feeling today?"

"I feel like I can take on the whole world today. After what we've been through nothing is going to stop me," answers Warren.

"Me too, me too, let's go and get on some rides, my folks gave me some money," Ernie says.

"Great I've got some too," replies Warren.

As they walk to the festival they run into Larry and Carry. The boys are all excited to see one another. The boys run off to get on some rides while Larry goes to see Pop Frankenstein.

"Look, The Spider, hey Ernie remember this ride from last year? We were too short to ride it last year," says Warren.
"Yea, let's go on it first," replies Ernie. The three boys buy their tickets and walk over to the rides entrance. They pass the creature with its arm sticking out saying you must be this tall to ride this ride. As they walk right past it with no problems, they all puff up their chest showing off for each other.

As they get off of the ride they see Beau, and Junior with all of his siblings standing near by talking with Pa Frankenstein and Larry.
"Hi Ernie, Warren and Carry, want to go on some rides with me? My dad won't let me go by myself, my brothers and sisters are all going with their friends and won't take me with them," says Junior. Of course the group says yes. All of the boys spend the rest of the morning riding all of the rides they can until their money runs out.

Warren invites his friends for a cookout that the Frankenstein's have every year during the festival. As the boys finish their lunch, Warren gets his broom out and all of the boys hurry to the north end of town to help Warren practice. It's always the safest place to go because no one ever goes there. He flies up and down the large open field and around some trees zigzagging in and out. Warren also practices swooping and stopping on a dime. All of his friends cheer him on. He flies over to Ernie, Carry and Junior.

"Wow, that was great. I never knew you had it in you." says Ernie. "It's hard to believe how much better you've gotten since our little trip."

"I learned so much more than just about flying," Warren says. They hear a loud horn blow, signaling that it's time for the race.

The boys get to the Gazebo in time to check in.

"Hey, Frankenstein are you going to show us some of your same tricks as last year. You know the ones where you crash into everything," laughs Henrietta Howard and some of her friends.

Someone taps the mike on the microphone and a loud squeal sounds out over the speakers, making most of the creatures cover their ears.

"Testing, testing, one, two, three. Would all creatures that are entered in the broom race please get into your positions. Remember both feet must be touching the ground or you will be disqualified. (The crowds start talking and making a lot of noise.) Please everyone be quiet, quiet while I give out the instructions please. The course is the same. You must go straight ahead until you reach the marker in the middle of Green Field, go around the outside of the pole then turn left. There is a row of trees that you must weave in and out of. The next obstacle is to go under the crooked tree. Then all the way

to Horse Shoe Rock, through the house shoe. After that
are a series of bars that you must then go over and under.
If you miss anything, points will be deducted. So even if
you get back to the finish line first, you could still lose
the race because of points. The first one back to the finish
line, and doesn't miss any obstacle, is the winner and will
win the grand prize. Remember this is state of the art,
years beyond itself, the Majestic IV Broomstick." says
Mr. Troll. The crowd applauds and yells with excitement.

"Wow, if only I could win that broom,everyone would
stop making fun of me." Warren thinks to himself.
Warren's friends give him the thumbs up wishing him
good luck.
"OK, get ready, on your mark, get set," yells Mr Troll.
Bang! The starting gun is shot off.

"And there off," says Tydous Swampthing, the local
famous radio announcer. Tydous is an average height
creature with brown weeds and moss hanging on him like
hair. He lives in a small wooden house on the west side
of the town in the marsh.
The announcements continue,
"It looks like Henrietta Howard is in the lead, she is a
young witch but with a lot of spunk. Look out for her, she
is a witch with a lot of talent. Second place looks like it's
Warlock Albert Schwartz. These two gave us quite a
show last year, maybe they will do it again this year. In
third place it is Warlock Sir William. What a surprise
folks, it's little Warren Frankenstein coming up from the
rear. I don't believe it he just took fourth place, (the

crowd goes wild). He barely finished last year, Warren sure has come a long way since then. They all go around the first pole and now the group is headed for the first obstacle. Henrietta is the first to zigzag around the trees, with Warlock Albert right on her heels. (The crowd screams with excitement.) Everyone else is making it through the tree obstacle one by one.

Oh oh, except little Homer Howard, it seams he does not quite have his older sister's talents, he's down. No, no, I spoke to soon, he's back up again and still in the race. Let's give him a big round of applause creatures. Now they are at the crooked tree and it looks like Witch Betty Black is moving up on Warren trying to take over fourth place. Each rider is dipping up and down through the tree. Oops, ("ooh,"") can be heard from the audience.) it looks like Warlock Elmer Stoned is out of the race, he dipped a little too low, ooh that's gotta hurt. Never fear first aid is on the way. The best battle is over fourth place, Witch Betty and Warren are really fighting it out. Remember folks, this race determines the Witches and Warlocks from the wanna Be's. Warlock Albert has taken over first place and is heading onto Horse Shoe Rock, Henrietta is close behind. This is a tough turn folks, they have to stay in between the two narrow rock walls that form the horseshoe shape. If they go too high it will be considered a missed obstacle, races have been lost over this turn. Creatures have also disappeared in this turn. The racers are coming out of the turn, it looks like, oh my yes they are. Albert is still in first place, Sir William has taken over second place. I don't believe it, Warren Frankenstein is in third place, and on a starter broom, with the training brooms still on. No one as young as him and with a starter broom has ever done so well. Unbelievable!(Warren's friends and family jump up and down screaming with delight.) What a race folks I have never seen anything like it before. But where is Henrietta, aah there she is, battling over fourth place with Witch Betty.

Oh my folks, Warren is making a move on Sir William. Remember Sir William is a three time champion of this race. What a bad place to move up on someone so close to an obstacle. But he has done it folks, Warren is in second place. (The crown screams!) Warren swoops right through the obstacle over and under like it's not even there. Warlock Albert is out in front, wow, look at Warren go, he is moving up fast on Albert. Look at that young boy go, he's is getting closer and closer, Wow! He did it! Warren has taken first place. He will have to work hard to keep it from the more experienced fliers." The crowd is going wild!. You can barely hear the announcer. No one can believe Warren has managed such a feat.

With the other witches and warlocks behind, Warlock Albert is trying desperately to catch up to Warren. He just can't seem to catch up with him. Warren has crossed the finish line first! Warren has the checkered flag." The crowd continues to scream with excitement. "Warren is the youngest creature to ever win this race!", yells Tydous into the microphone. The rest of the competitors swoop in over the finish line claiming their place. The judges put their heads together as they total the scores. The envelope is given to Tydous. He clears his throat as he leans into the mike asking everyone to be quiet.

"In Fourth Place is Witch Betty!" She takes her place near the stand, the crowd applause as the officials give her her prize then shakes her hand and congratulate her. "In third Place is Sir William!" The same ceremony is performed with William as it was with Betty.

"Second place goes to Warlock Albert Schwartz!" The crowd gets louder with their applause and yells. The judges give Albert his prize and congratulate him. "What you all have been waiting for, the First Place winner not only set a new time record, but he also is the youngest and only creature to ever win this event on a training broom! Warren Frankenstein is our Grand Prize Winner!"

The crowd screams with excitement, as Warren moves toward his place with the others, people try to touch him and slap him on the back. Tears form in Warren's eyes. Witch Hazel walks up to Warren with his new broomstick. Tydous holds the microphone to Hazel's mouth, as she speaks. "Warren you have been a good student of mine. You have worked harder than anyone ever has trying to become a Warlock. Even though you had a lot of things going against you, you never quit. So it gives me great pleasure to give you your new broom, The Majestic IV. May you ride it with great pleasure and as the Great Warlock that you are." The crowd screams and applauds as Warren takes the broom into his hands.

Warren looks over the wonderful broomstick that he has been dreaming of owning, since the first day he saw it in Mr. Trolls shop. He caresses it as he runs his hands over the smooth lines of the broomstick. Warren looks over at his old broomstick, then he looks up at Witch Hazel.

With a tear running down his cheek, Warren clears his throat. Warren beings to speak "I thought owning this broomstick would solve all of my problems. It has been the only thing that I have wanted since the first day that I saw it in Mr. Trolls shop. But I am not worthy of owning such a magnificent broomstick. It should go to the only person who deserves it. She showed me how I can achieve anything that I want to as long as I keep trying. Witch Hazel, thank you for everything that you have done for me." With that, Warren hands the broom back over to Witch Hazel. She accepts it with shaking hands and a tear running down her cheek. To be given a broomstick is the greatest honor that can be bestowed upon a warlock or a witch. Witch Hazel leans over and kisses Warren on the forehead. Then mouths the words, thank you, for she is too choked up to speak. As she stands up, Warren notices that the witch has his training broomstick in her hand. Harry runs up the small broomstick, on up Hazel's arm until he reaches her shoulder. Witch Hazel leans her new broomstick up against Harry. She then takes the small training broom into both hands and throws it up into the air. The grateful witch says some magic words and waves her hands.

Warren,s broom begins to spin around and around. It

spins so fast you can hardly see it. Then it shoots high up into the air with a trail of sparkling lights as if someone shot off a large rocket. All of a sudden there is a large boom that seems to shake the earth. Then beautiful fire works of all colors, shapes and sizes fill the sky. The crowd applauds at the beautiful sight. Slowly you can begin to see something coming from the sky heading straight toward Warren. It swoops down and stops right in front of Warren. Its is the most wonderful broomstick that Warren has ever seen. The finish is a shinny red lacquer and the bristles look like they are on fire.

Warren makes eye contact with the old witch, she gives him a nod and a wink. He reaches out to touch the broomstick with a shaky hand, as he wraps his small fingers around the broomstick he can feel the power that it holds. The young boy and the old witch give each other a hug as they stand side by side each other holding up their prizes in the air with one hand. The crowd screams and claps theirs hands as hard as they can.

Tydous yells into the mike, "The best race ever folks, the best race ever!"

Chapter 9
Believe

As Warren moves through the crowd at the festival people keep patting him on the back and congratulating him. Over the intercom the talent show is announced. The crowd makes their way over to the pavilion where the show is to be held. Tydous is always the master of ceremonies at these events. "Gather around folks, pull up your chairs, it's time for the greatest show on earth!" he yells into the microphone. The crowd moves in around the pavilion, everyone is talking with excitement. They all arrange their lawn chairs, kitchen chairs and blankets so they can see the front of the stage.

"Quiet everyone, please, quiet!" Tydous yells into the mic as he holds his hands up waving them to get everyone's attention. "Our judges for this evening will be the first witch among witch's, the one, the only, Witch Hazel and of course Harry the spider!" The crowd claps their hands. The next judge will make you a deal that you just can't refuse. Why it's Mr. J. R. Troll, the crowd claps louder. Last, but not least, is the one and only Mayor and ancestor of the founder of our great town, Mayor Frankenstein. The large crowd really roars with applause now.

"The first act truly shines only at night and will tap dance you into a hypnotic state. Please welcome Count Emile Dracula!" The crowd cheers as the Count taps across the stage to Tip Toe Through the Tulips. When the Count finishes, Tydous walks back onto the stage clapping his hands and motioning everyone to do the same. "Our next act is a brother and sister act, they are going to delight you with their ability to play the flute and the violin. Please help me give a big welcome to the Howard Kids." The two youngsters take their place on the stage. As they play they make more sour notes and squeals so you can hardly tell what they are playing. But the crowd gives them a big round of applause. There seems to be one bad act after another, but everyone is having such a good time it doesn't seem to matter.

At last The Beasts are up, Warren never really paid any attention to his brother's group when they practiced. It always just sounded like a lot of banging around to him. The emcee announces them, the curtains open up and they start playing their instruments and singing. The crowd just loves it and starts dancing in the isles singing along with them. The judges all lean toward each other talking between themselves and nodding their heads.

As the group finishes, Tydous walks onto the stage and motions for the teens to stay there. He walks over to the judges and gets an envelope. Tydous yells into the mic, "Creatures one and all, the judges have come to an unanimous decision. But first, lets start with Third Place, for a free hair cut at Wolfman's Barber Shop is Emile Dracula with his tap,tap, tapping shoes!", everyone claps. "Second Place winner gets dinner for two at the Little Wicked Witch's Diner. The winner of this prize is Bertha

Black and her flaming batons!", everyone claps their hands. "The winner by a land slide for the 100pcs of gold coins and a chance to record a CD, are the Beasts!"

Everyone goes wild and begs for an encore, so the group starts playing another song. Again the crowd is up on their feet singing and dancing. After a couple of more songs, Mayor Frankenstein gets up and announces, " Just one more song, I will never get my kids to bed as it is." The crowd roars with laughter, but break up and head home after the song is finished.

In class the next morning, most of the kids are talking about all of the excitement over the three days. Teachers are having a hard time getting the kids to settle down to begin each class.

Warren has a new outlook on things. He no longer feels inadequate. In science class, Professor Madd watches Warren carefully as he mixes his potion. Warren with his new self confidence mixes it with no problems at all and gets the exact reaction that is necessary.

Warren was able to get to his next class on time. Mrs. Wolfgang is surprised to see him.
"Warren did you have lab today in Madd's potion class?"
"Yes Mrs. Wolfgang." answers Warren.

Just a little confidence can go a long way

The end.

"Illegal Aliens, New Beginning"

As Faithe runs onto the long gangplank, someone is banging loudly on the door from the control room. It startles Faithe, and as she turns to look she trips and falls, she screams, rolls, and falls over the edge of the gangplank.

She manages to grab a support for the railing. Faithe is barely hanging on with her hands for dear life. Her entire body is dangling into the darkness of the deep hole. The young girl can feel the heat from the exhaust coming up from the bottom of the space craft.

Available on AMAZON.COM

"Illegal Aliens, Building a Home"

The night is so dark and still, all you can hear are the waves as they gently slap up against the boats that are docked. Plus with no moon tonight the extra darkness will be a great cover for the young alien heroes. However there is a glow from an overhead light on a pole next to the gangplank. Luckily it does not throw very much light on to the large yacht. Maverick slowly climbs up the side of the boat. He managed to throw a rope up over the railing, with a small grappling hook to anchor it with. As Maverick peeks up over the edge of the ship he can't see anyone, so he quietly slips onto the boat. Dutch follows him and does the exact same thing. Suddenly they can hear foot steps coming closer toward them, so they duck down in the shadows. A man holding a rifle walks within a couple of inches of the two boys. When the man turns his back toward them, Dutch shoots the man with a dart. The gunman grabs the back of his neck and starts to curse, he sways. As the man begins to fall, Maverick jumps up and grabs him and his rifle. Making sure they don't hit the deck and make any noise.

Available on AMAZON.COM

Coming soon, look for these titles;

"The Camel Without a Hump"

"Where the Road Takes You"

"Creatureville, Saving Doctor Frankenstein"

"Juror Number 11"